For Rob K.K.
To all the Swithenbanks, with love J.P.

Text copyright © 2000 Kay Kinnear
Illustrations copyright © 2000 Julie Park
This edition copyright © 2000 Lion Publishing

The moral rights of the author and illustrator
have been asserted

Published by
Lion Publishing plc
Sandy Lane West, Oxford, England
www.lion-publishing.co.uk
ISBN 0 7459 4211 3 (hardback)
ISBN 0 7459 4443 4 (paperback)

First hardback edition 2000
10 9 8 7 6 5 4 3 2 1 0
First paperback edition 2000
10 9 8 7 6 5 4 3 2 1

A catalogue record for this book is available
from the British Library

Typeset in 20/26 Latin 725 BT
Printed and bound in Singapore

Deedee's Easter Surprise

Kay Kinnear
Illustrations by Julie Park

LION
Children's Books

Deedee and Jack were the best of friends.
Jack thought she was the most
wonderful duck in the whole world.

Deedee followed Jack everywhere.
Deedee followed Jack when he helped
his mum feed the hens.

Deedee went to the field when
Jack helped his dad plant potatoes.

Deedee sat on Jack's lap
when he watched TV.

At night Deedee settled
down in her box in the porch.

ZZZZZZZ

In spring Mum said, 'Soon Deedee will find a mate and lay eggs and have baby ducks.'

'Deedee doesn't like other ducks,' said Jack. 'She only likes me.'

I taught Deedee to swim.

I taught Deedee to dive.

I taught Deedee to talk.

Quack, quack!

Quack!

'Deedee won't leave me,' said Jack.
Deedee was his best friend.

One day Jack's mum said, 'It's nearly Easter.'
So they collected some eggs from the hens
to make special Easter eggs. They were going
to take them to nursery school for an egg hunt.

First, Mum boiled the eggs. Then Jack dyed them. Deedee watched from her box in the porch.

'Can we take Deedee tomorrow?' asked Jack. 'She wants to see my school.'

'Maybe,' said Mum. 'I'll phone your teacher and ask.'

Jack took Deedee to school the next day.
'She's a lovely duck,' said Miss Webb.
'I showed her how to talk,' said Jack.
'Talk, Deedee!'

While Miss Webb hid the Easter eggs outside, Jack's mum read a story.

It was about the very first Easter. A man called Jesus had died, and his friends were very sad.

I'd be sad too.

But Jesus came back! God sent an angel to tell them that he was alive again.

'Did his friends see him?' asked Jack.
'Yes, lots of times,' said Mum.

The children hurried outside for the egg hunt.
They ran and shouted and laughed.
Hunting for Easter eggs was fun.

They peeped inside the playhouse and under the slide.

Jack grabbed his mum's hand and said, 'Look, Mum, look at my green one!'

Everyone found an egg.

When it was home time, the mums and dads came to fetch their children.

Jack wanted to show Deedee his green egg,
but he couldn't see her anywhere.
'DEEDEE! DEEDEE! DEEDEE!' he called.
'All that shouting scared her,' said Mum.
'She must have flown home.'

On the way home it started to rain. Then Jack dropped his Easter egg.

Everything had gone wrong. And he'd forgotten to look after Deedee. He began to cry.

'Don't worry, love. We can make more eggs,' said Mum.

'We can't make a new Deedee,' sobbed Jack.

Oh no!

When they got home, Jack rushed to look for Deedee. But she wasn't in her box.

Jack stood in the porch watching and waiting for her.

'She's lost,' he whispered to himself.

When it stopped raining,
Jack and his dad went to search
for Deedee.
'She's probably by the pond
with the other ducks,' said Dad.
But she wasn't there.

She wasn't with the hens.

She wasn't in the shed
with the tractor.

They looked all
round the farm but
she wasn't *anywhere*.

Jack was very worried. Deedee
had never, ever gone away before.

When it was bedtime, Jack went upstairs to his room.

And who should be waiting for him but Deedee! She was snuggled on top of his sweatshirt.

'Look, Mum!' shouted Jack. 'She's come back!'
'Clever Deedee,' said Mum, 'she must have
flown in through the window.'
Deedee had never been upstairs before, but
Mum said she could stay just this once.

Jack picked up Deedee and gave her a hug.
Then he saw the egg!

It wasn't an egg from the egg hunt. It was
Deedee's egg.

'Deedee's made me a new egg!' cried Jack.

'What a lovely surprise! And just in time
for Easter,' said Mum.

And the surprise just got bigger...

and bigger...

and better...

and better!

Quack, quack!